MARTHA SPEAKS™

A Pup's Tale

Adaptation by Jamie White

Based on a TV series teleplay written by Allan Neuwirth

Based on the characters created by Susan Meddaugh

HOUGHTON MIFFLIN HARCOURT

Boston · New York · 2010

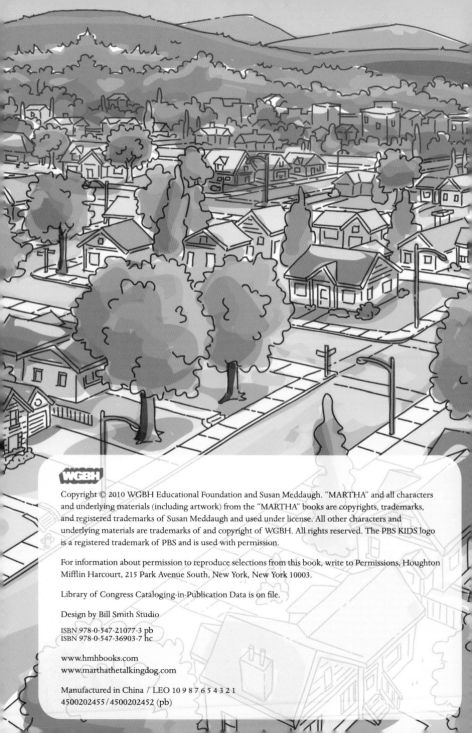

For information about permission to reproduce selections from this book, write to Permissions, Houghton
Mifflin Harcourt, 215 Park Avenue South, New York, New York 10003.

Library of Congress Cataloging-in-Publication Data is on file.

Design by Bill Smith Studio

ISBN 978-0-547-21077-3 pb
ISBN 978-0-547-36903-7 hc

www.hmhbooks.com
www.marthathetalkingdog.com

Manufactured in China / LEO 10 9 8 7 6 5 4 3 2 1
4500202455 / 4500202452 (pb)

MARTHA SAYS HELLO

Hi there!

Be warned, Martha fans: What you are about to read might shock you!

You already know that Martha is a dog who can speak. And speak and speak . . .

And you probably know that she's been able to speak ever since Helen fed her alphabet soup. No one's sure how or why, but the letters in the soup traveled up to Martha's brain instead of down to her stomach.

Now, as long as she eats her daily bowl of alphabet soup, she can talk. To her family: Helen, baby Jake, Mom, Dad, and their dog Skits, who only speaks Dog. To Helen's friend Truman. To anyone who'll listen.

Sometimes Martha's family wishes she didn't talk *quite* so much.

But who would want to discourage a talking dog from, well, talking? Besides, her speaking comes in handy. One night, she called 911 to stop a burglar.

So, do you think you know all about Martha? Well, think again. This is the surprising story about Martha's early life in crime.

Sit, stay, and hear all about it . . .

WHO KNEW?

Martha's good friend Truman didn't know this shocking tale. And he knows *everything!*

It happened like this. Martha and Truman were watching TV at his house. On screen, police chased the bad guys.

"Those crooks aren't very smart," said Truman. "It won't take long for the cops to catch them."

"They always do," said Martha. "Just like they caught me back when I was robbing stores."

Truman's jaw dropped. "Robbing *what?*"

"Stores," said Martha. "Before Helen adopted me, I robbed stores. Well, one store . . . and a museum."

She stood up and yawned.

"I'm off to the park," she said, heading to the front door. "Those ducks don't bark at themselves."

"A store? A *museum?* Robbery? When were you going to tell me this?"

"It never came up," said Martha. "Maybe one day I'll write my life story. Then I'll tell everyone."

"You're going to write your autobiography?" asked Truman.

"No, my life story," said Martha.

"That's what an autobiography is—a book someone writes about her own life. Can I help you write it? Starting with your life in crime?"

"I guess," said Martha. "If you don't mind barking at a few ducks first."

So that's just what they did. They went to the park and barked at ducks.

And then Truman helped Martha write this book. Martha talked. Truman wrote.

Now go on . . . read her surprising autobiography.

MY LIFE IN CRIME
BY MARTHA

I was only eight weeks old, and already behind bars . . . at the animal shelter.

Every day, I sat in my small cage waiting to be adopted. I'd watch humans walk in and out of the animal shelter. But no one wanted to take me home.

Kazuo was in charge of the shelter, just like he is now. He tried to find us dogs good homes. Sometimes he'd point me out to visitors. The first one I remember well was a lady in a fur coat.

How could I forget her? She tried to stuff me into her purse. *Ouch!* I was too big.

"I need a dog that fits!" yelled the lady.

And thankfully she moved on—to the next cage.

The next day, a grumpy man visited.

"I'd like a dog that can do tricks," he said.

I danced in circles for him.

"Is that all it can do?" asked the man.

He moved on, too.

Later, a magician came in. He squeezed me into his top hat. Then he tried to pull me out by my ears. I yelped. *Ouch* again!

"Will her ears grow?" asked the magician.

"Dude," said Kazuo, taking me back from the magician.

"I think you need a *rabbit*."

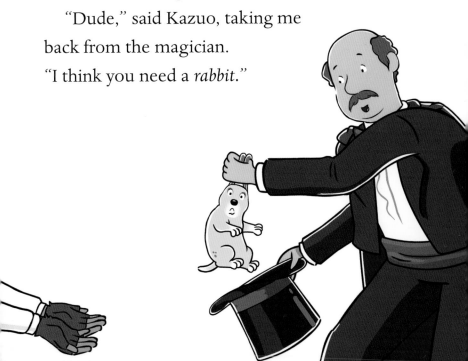

No one thought I was just right.

All day long, I'd watch pets leave with new owners.

"Give me a chance!" I wanted to shout. "I'll be the best pet on four legs!"

But I couldn't speak. I hadn't eaten alphabet soup yet.

"Don't give up hope, Martha," Kazuo said. "There are still lots of possibilities."

I cocked my head to the side. *Huh?*

"Possibilities are things that can happen," said Kazuo.

At that point, the only possibility I saw was a lifetime behind bars.

"Lots of people want dogs," said Kazuo. "It's possible you might be a police dog."

A K-9 cop! I could just imagine it. I'd direct traffic with my tail and my whistle. There would never be a traffic jam!

"That's just *one* possibility," Kazuo said. "It's also possible you could be a water rescue dog."

Hot dog! I thought. I'd put a stop to any dangerous water tricks. Besides, everyone looks up to a lifeguard.

"Or it's possible you could live with the owner of a bowling alley. You could put your keen sense of smell to use."

Yes! I'd work at the shoe rental desk. When people returned their bowling shoes, I'd sniff out their sneakers for them.

These possibilities all sounded great. But none of them was what I really, *really* wanted. What I yearned for was a home and family of my own.

Then one morning, things began to look promising.

THE LITTLE RED-HAIRED GIRL

It all started when a family visited the animal shelter, looking for a pet.

"A cat?" Kazuo said. "We have plenty. Follow me."

The grownups walked past my cage. But the little girl stopped. She had the nicest smile.

"Hi!" she said.

The moment I saw her, my tail wagged with joy. Can you guess who she was?

17

"Helen!" her mom called from across the room.

Yes, she was my very own Helen!

Mom pointed at an orange cat. "Look. Isn't he cute?"

"I guess," said Helen. "But look at this puppy!"

Could she be my new owner? I gave her cheek a slobbery kiss.

"That's Martha," said Kazuo.

"Martha!" said Helen. "I like her. Let's adopt her!"

"But honey," said Dad, "that's not a cat."

"She's better than a cat," said Helen.

I knew then that this was a girl after my own heart.

"Helen," said Mom, walking over. "We've discussed this. Don't you recall? Dogs need a lot of care."

"Yes, but . . ."

Mom placed a hand on Helen's shoulder. "I'm sorry. Martha looks sweet, but a puppy is too much work right now."

Now things *didn't* look promising. And they were about to get worse. A *lot* worse.

A SHOEBOX-SIZE DOG

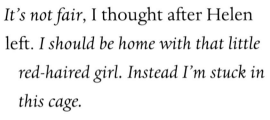

It's not fair, I thought after Helen left. *I should be home with that little red-haired girl. Instead I'm stuck in this cage.*

The shelter was quiet. The animals snoozed. Behind his counter, Kazuo read a magazine. The peace didn't last long.

A lady wearing a purple dress and lots of jewelry burst through the door. She was with a man in a suit. The man was quiet. The lady was not.

20

She wore plastic bangles that rattled when she moved her arms. She spoke in a loud voice. And although Kazuo was right in front of her nose, she banged the desk bell.

DING!

Kazuo jumped.

Ding! Ding!

"Excuse me—do you work here?" the lady demanded.

Kazuo looked around. "Uh . . . yes?"

"Carlotta Bumblecrumb!" the woman said, introducing herself.

"What can I do for you, Ms. Crumble-bum?" asked Kazuo.

"It's *Bumblecrumb!*" she snapped. "I'm here to adopt a dog. It should be the size of a shoebox."

"Hmm," said Kazuo. "Follow me."

Kazuo tried to show her a poodle. But she peeked into my cage.

"You look promising," she said to me. "And when I say you look promising, I mean I think you'll work out just right."

She read my nametag. "Can 'Martha'
be trained?"

"Trained to do what?" asked Kazuo.

"None of your—" began the lady. She
slapped her hand over her mouth. "*Oops!* I
mean . . . I recall that as a child I owned a dog
that did tricks. Ever since then, I've yearned
for another."

Kazuo raised an eyebrow. "Why does Martha need to be the size of a shoebox?"

"So I can push the mutt through a hole about—*oops!*" said Carlotta Bumblecrumb. Again she stopped midsentence. "I mean . . . because I've already built a tiny doghouse. Yes, I built it out of a *shoebox*. I need a pooch that will fit inside."

"You know she's going to grow, right?" said Kazuo.

"Then I'll build a bigger doghouse," she said. "How much do you want for her?"

"We don't charge you to adopt a pet."

"Perfect," she said.

She opened my cage. *Rattle, rattle* went her bangles. Her hands reached for me.

At that moment, I yearned to speak Human. "Consider the cat!" I'd say. "Cats fit perfectly into shoeboxes! Think it over, lady!"

I backed away, and Kazuo noticed.

"Uh, I just recalled something," he said
quickly. "Martha hasn't had all her shots yet.
You'll have to come back in a few weeks."

Carlotta Bumblecrumb scowled.

"I see," she said, forcing a smile. She waved
goodbye to me. "Ta ta then, sweet cheeks!
Mama will be back soon!"

With that, luckily, the loud scary lady and
her silent companion left. Kazuo and I let out
a sigh. Phew.

But I was still sad and alone. And I wasn't the only one. At home, Helen was heartbroken, too.

I know what you're thinking. How can I narrate Helen's side of the story if I wasn't there? Well, Helen told it to me. So now I can narrate it for you . . .

DOGGY NIGHTMARE

"Please, please, please!" Helen begged. She hopped in front of the sofa, where her mother was trying to read. "I promise I'll take care of the puppy!"

Mom put down her book.

"That's what you said about Goldie," she said. "Do you recall what happened to her?"

When Helen was five, she had a goldfish named Goldie. All day long, Goldie did nothing but swim in circles. Around and around the fishbowl she went.

Goldie looks bored, Helen thought. *She needs a vacation.*

So the next time Helen's family went to the lake, Helen secretly brought Goldie along, too. *Plop!* She dropped Goldie into the water for a quick swim. After a few minutes, Helen said, "Come back now, fishy." But Helen never saw Goldie again.

(This scene from Helen's past is what Truman calls a flashback. But if he doesn't stop interrupting me to explain what a word means, I'll never finish my story!)

"I didn't know Goldie wouldn't come back," Helen told Mom. "I'll be more careful with a dog. *Please?*"

"Helen, we went over this at the shelter today," said Mom. "A dog is a big responsibility. You need to wash it, walk it . . ."

"I'll wash her. I'll walk her," said Helen, hopping higher. "*Pleeeeease?*"

"No," said Mom. "I'm sorry."

Helen stopped hopping. As the days passed, she stopped begging, too. She didn't stop missing me, though. One look at the refrigerator door would tell you that. It was covered with her drawings of me.

One day, Helen began to write my name
on her latest picture. Mom and Dad watched
from the doorway.

"How do you spell 'Martha'?" asked Helen.
Mom looked at Dad. "I give up," she said.
Dad nodded.

Helen's face lit up. "Do you mean—?"

"Yes," said Mom, smiling. "You can have Martha."

"THANK YOU!" shouted Helen.

She hugged Mom's legs. She threw her arms into the air. She ran in circles through the house.

"YAY! WHOO-HOO! YIPPEEEEEEEE!"

Mom and Dad covered their ears.

"We'd better go first thing in the morning," Dad said.

The next morning at the shelter, I lay in
my cage, watching a collie eat kibble. *Ho-hum.*
Bor-ing.

But then . . . Kazuo ran in wearing a smile.

"GUESS WHAT, MARTHA?" he shouted.
"YOU'RE BEING ADOPTED!"

Holy macaroni! Those were the sweetest
words I'd ever heard. I leaped to my paws.
That little red-haired girl had come
back for me!

Or so I thought.

Kazuo pointed to the doorway.
"Martha, say hello to your new
owner, Miss Eudora Biddlecomb!"

My tail stopped wagging.

Eudora Biddlecomb was no little red-haired girl.

"Hello, sweet little poochie," she said in a shaky old lady's voice. She tickled me under the chin. "We're going to be pals, you and I. Hee hee hee. I knew I liked you before."

Kazuo raised his eyebrows. "Before?"

The old lady's hand covered her mouth.

"*Oops!* I mean . . . before I came in. I had a feeling I'd like what I saw here," she said, winking at me. "And I was right. I'm going to love owning you."

Before I could even woof goodbye to Kazuo, the old lady whisked me out the door. Suddenly she didn't need to lean on her cane anymore. Like an Olympic runner, she hustled us into a pink limo parked outside.

"Good poochie," she said, slamming the car door.

Just before it shut, I saw an awful sight. Helen and her parents were walking into the shelter! I had missed them by seconds.

"ARF!" I barked. "ARF! ARF!"

"QUIET!" shouted the old lady.

Her voice was different. It was familiar. It was LOUD.

Eudora Biddlecomb took off her gray wig.

"Ha! Surprised to see me again?" said Carlotta Bumblecrumb. "You're mine now. Tomorrow you start working for me."

This was a doggy nightmare. Even worse than the one I had about being chased by a giant head of lettuce.

"Home, Mr. Stubble!" she ordered the driver.

I scratched at the back window and watched Helen disappear. Of all the promising possibilities I had imagined, this was not how I thought I'd end up.

HOME HORRIBLE HOME

At the shelter, Helen stood next to my empty cage. (I'm narrating Helen's story again. Can you tell?)

"She's . . . gone?" asked Helen, her voice trembling.

"I'm sorry," said Kazuo. "I wish you'd arrived sooner."

"Martha," Helen said softly.

She felt like she was about to cry. And then she did.

Meanwhile, where was *I*?

I was lying on the cold floor of Carlotta
Bumblecrumb and Mr. Stubble's warehouse.
My new home wasn't exactly what I'd hoped
for. There was no comfy couch. No chewies.
No chops. And no Helen.

Instead I saw a broken table, hard chairs, an
old TV, and boarded-up windows.

"Time to begin your training, pooch!" said
Carlotta Bumblecrumb. She took a red ball
from her purse. "See this? When I throw it,
you're going to fetch it. Got that?"

She threw the ball. "Fetch!"

I watched it bounce away. *Why does she want me to fetch that little red ball?* I wondered.

"Go on!" she ordered. "It's a game. FETCH THE BALL!"

Let's play another game, I wanted to say. *How about "Fetch the MEATball"?*

"Mr. Stubble, show this mutt how it's done!" said Carlotta Bumblecrumb.

She tossed another ball.

"Watch this, pooch," she said. "First, he'll run. Second, he'll get the ball. Finally, he'll bring it back to me! A proper sequence, see?"

Mr. Stubble ran on all fours with his tongue hanging out. He fetched the ball with his mouth. He looked like a very silly dog.

"Good boy, Mr. Stubble!" she said.

She popped a cookie into his mouth.

Hey! Nobody said anything about cookies, I thought. *That's a whole new ball game. Maybe fetching could be fun.*

"Fetch!" ordered Carlotta Bumblecrumb, throwing the ball again.

I ran in front of Mr. Stubble. I got the ball. I returned it.

"Excellent! Good dog!" she said, giving me a cookie.

Mmm, tasty. Fetching isn't so bad, I thought as I chomped. *But what are these two really up to?*

It didn't take long to find out.

OUR FIRST HIT

"Here it is, Mr. Stubble," whispered Carlotta Bumblecrumb. "Thousands of dollars in rare sports junk. Soon it will be ours!"

We peered into the dark window of the sports collectibles store. Inside were balls, shirts, and photos, all signed by sports stars.

Why are we here? I wondered. *It's bedtime. The store is closed. Besides, these two don't seem like sports fans.*

Carlotta Bumblecrumb opened the store's mail slot. It was exactly the size of a shoebox.

"In you go," she said as Mr. Stubble squeezed me though the slot. "You see? Perfect fit!"

She peeked in at me. "Now fetch the ball!"

I sniffed around. Where was the red ball?

Carlotta Bumblecrumb and Mr. Stubble tapped at the window.

I heard her muffled voice. "Fetch the ball there!" she said. "The one that's signed by Babe Ruth!"

She pointed to a white ball on a stand.

Babe Ruth? I thought. *Wow. This Ruth must be a special babe. Not many babies can sign their names.*

I leaped up to grab the ball with my mouth. *Whoops!* I missed.

I tried again . . . *nope!*

I jumped as high as I could, and crashed to the floor. THUD.

But above me, the stand teetered. The baseball wobbled and fell. It bounced off my head with a *clunk. Ow!* Where did it go?

And what was that loud, terrible sound? It went *WOO WOO WOO WOO*.

The burglar alarm had gone off. But I didn't worry. I didn't know about alarms then. I only knew that I was close to getting a cookie. I had spotted the ball again.

"THERE! GOOD DOG!" Carlotta Bumblecrumb cheered. "Bring it here!"

I pounced on the ball. I chewed it. I rolled it. I chewed it some more. Fetching was so much fun.

"NO, NO, NO!" shouted Carlotta
Bumblecrumb. She looked angry.

What's the matter? I wondered.

A moment later, she peeked into the slot.
She didn't look mad anymore. She held a
cookie out for me.

"Come here with the ball. Nice doggy,"
she said.

I brought the ball to her. *Cookie time!*
Or not.

"Got you, you mangy mutt!" she said,
grabbing my collar. She did *not* have the
cookie anymore. (I would have smelled it.)
She yanked me back through the slot and
took the ball.

"It's mine!" she cried, holding it up. "It's
mine! It's . . . *covered in doggy drool?* Ew!"

Down the street, police sirens wailed.

"Let's get out of here!"

The limo's tires screeched as we made our getaway.

"Lost them! Hee hee hee," said Carlotta Bumblecrumb. "Mr. Stubble, turn here! We're meeting someone."

He pulled into a dark alley. We stepped out.

A man stood in the shadows. His shoulders twitched. He kept looking back and forth.

"Nervous Ned?" asked Carlotta Bumblecrumb.

"Y-y-y-yes!" said Nervous Ned, jumping in surprise. "How did you know?"

"Just a hunch," she said. "I have the item we discussed. A 1934 baseball signed by Babe Ruth!"

She handed him the ball.

"Nice work, Stumblebum," said Nervous Ned.

"It's *Bumblecrumb!*"

Nervous Ned inspected the ball.

"Wait a minute," he said. "This doesn't say Babe Ruth. It says Blaaghh Rumff."

He pointed to the smudged signature.

Carlotta Bumblecrumb tore the ball from his hands. "It has a little slobber on it, that's all," she said. "This ball is worth a small fortune."

"It's worth something *small* all right," said Nervous Ned. "Like a dime."

Desperately she held me up.

"Then how about an autographed pooch?" she said. "See, her tongue says Babe Ruth, uh . . ."

I stuck out my tongue.

"Backwards," she said.

But Nervous Ned wasn't interested.

CATNAPPING

Our first robbery was a bust. It was back to the warehouse for us. I dozed in my crate while Mr. Stubble read a newspaper. Carlotta Bumblecrumb paced.

"A perfect plan ruined by dog drool!" she said. She pounded the table with her fist. "I had aspirations, you know."

Mr. Stubble looked confused.

"Aspirations, Mr. Stubble!" she said. "Aspirations are things you really want to do. I aspired to be rich. But here I am, wearing cheap plastic jewelry. It's not fair."

Mr. Stubble returned to reading his newspaper. Suddenly he gasped.

"What is it?" she said.

Mr. Stubble pointed to a photo of a fat white cat sitting on a giant can of cat food. Carlotta Bumblecrumb snatched the paper away from him.

"Wagstaff City is proud to welcome Jingles, the famous dancing cat from the Krazy Kitty Cat Food commercials," she read. "He will be staying at our own Come-On-Inn for the next three days."

Back then, the Come-On-Inn didn't allow pets. (How rude!) But Jingles was not your average kitty. He was a VIC, a Very Important Cat.

Carlotta Bumblecrumb's eyes twinkled. "That hip-hopping furball is worth millions! I wish I could get my hands on him."

She cast me a sly look.

"And maybe I can!" she said.

Turns out she had a plan. We tried it the very next day. The *first* part of it worked . . .

NO PETS ALLOWED, warned the Come-On-Inn's sign.

And yet there I was.

But if you were at the inn, you wouldn't have seen me. You'd have seen a lady wearing a room service uniform and plastic jewelry, pushing a cart down a hall. On the cart was a dish topped with a domed food cover.

You wouldn't have seen Mr. Stubble either, but he was there too. He hid under the draping tablecloth. As for me, I was under the food cover on the top of the cart. It was dark under there, but it smelled good.

Mmm, bacon! I thought. *But where is it?*

The cart came to a stop.

"We're at the cat's room," she whispered.
"Do we have a surprise for kitty! Hee hee
hee."

She knocked on the door.

"Complimentary room service!" she called.

The door creaked open.

"Oh, goody!" said the man who was
Jingles's owner. "Please come in."

Carlotta Bumblecrumb rolled the cart
across the room.

"Here you are, kitty! A yummy treat just for . . . YOU!" she said, whipping the cover off me.

I blinked in the light.

Inches away from me, Jingles was curled up on a fancy chair. He stared at me in mild surprise.

"MEOW?"

"RUFF?" I responded.

"Go!" my new owner cried. "Chase the cat! Chase the cat! The—"

Cat? I thought. *But I want bacon!*

I begged on my hind legs. *Bacon, bacon, PLEASE?*

Carlotta Bumblecrumb groaned.

"Never mind!" she said. "Mr. Stubble, NOW!"

Mr. Stubble stumbled out from the bottom of the cart. But he accidentally took the tablecloth *and me* with him. He looked like a ghost wearing a dog as a hat.

"Get going!" yelled Carlotta Bumblecrumb. She grabbed the tablecloth to pull it off him. Mr. Stubble tripped and knocked her off her feet. They landed in a heap. The tablecloth had them tied up like a package.

From his chair, Jingles watched us. His eyes narrowed. Then he snarled. This was not good.

Jingles's owner hollered. Furniture crashed. Glass shattered. Finally we all exploded out of the room.

Jingles chased us down the hall and around the inn. Boy, that fat cat could run.

(And that's just *one* reason why cats are not my favorite people.)

A BONEHEADED PLAN

After the Jingles cat-astrophe, we returned to
the hideout. Mr. Stubble played jacks. Carlotta
Bumblecrumb watched TV. They were
supposed to be planning our next move. But
they were too sore. They were covered in cat
scratches.

Jingles really got them, I thought. And then

there he was again! On
TV, he hip-hop danced on
a giant can of Krazy Kitty
Cat Food.

"Bah!" said Carlotta Bumblecrumb. "When I reflect on my life, Mr. Stubble—"

He looked confused, as if he were about to ask a question.

She rolled her eyes. "*Reflecting* means thinking carefully and remembering. When I reflect on my life, I wonder where I went wrong."

She sighed and changed the channel.

"And now," said a TV announcer, "the Museum Network presents *Dinosaurs on Display!*"

"Who cares about a bunch of dusty old bones?" she said.

But Mr. Stubble's eyes lit up, and he pointed at me.

"That's it!" she exclaimed. "We've been going about this all wrong! The pooch should be doing what dogs do naturally. Fetching BONES!"

Something told me fetching bones wasn't going to be as promising as it sounded.

It turns out Carlotta Bumblecrumb had a BIG idea. We were about to commit a dino-size crime.

We waited until night fell. In the moonlight, we crept along the roof of the Museum of Natural History. The skylight on the roof gave us a view into the museum below. Inside was what looked like a giant tower of bones. It was an all-you-can-chew bone buffet!

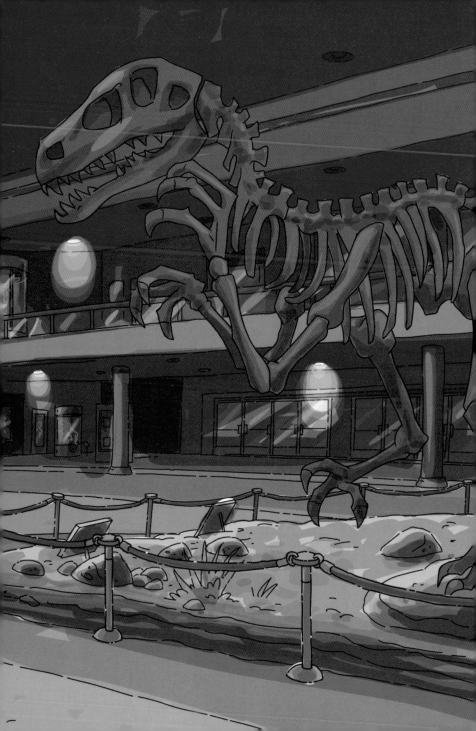

"There it is, the T. rex!" said Carlotta
Bumblecrumb. "I'm done reminiscing, Mr.
Stubble. No more thinking and talking about
the past. The past is about to make us rich!
We'll steal that dinosaur, even if we have to
do it one bone at a time."

Mr. Stubble pried the window open.

"Okay, pooch," she said. "Your job is very
simple. Fetch the bones. Got it?"

I nodded. *My pleasure!*

Mr. Stubble tied a rope around
me. He tied the other end to a
ventilation pipe. Then he slipped
me through the open window.
I dropped lower and lower,
until . . . I stopped
in midair.

"We're caught in the
rope, Mr. Stubble!"
I heard Carlotta
Bumblecrumb yell
from above. "Turn this
way! Lift your leg. NO!
Other leg!"

Meanwhile I was
swinging around like a yo-yo on a string.

"Turn around, you clumsy—argh!
WAIT! I'll do it!"

Finally, I was lowered to the museum floor. I had been looking forward to the bone buffet, but as soon as my paws hit the ground, I lost my appetite. I longed to go back up to the roof.

That T. rex looked a million times bigger from the ground. Its jaws were open. Its teeth were huge. And it looked like it hadn't eaten for a long *long* time.

Gulp! *I'm about to be a dino snack,* I thought.

BUSTING BUFFOONS

"It's just a bunch of bones!" Carlotta Bumblecrumb called down. "Fetch them!"

Slooooowly, I crept over to the dinosaur. I concentrated on the foot, not the mouth. Up close, it didn't look so scary. It looked kind of . . . *delicious*.

I chomped down on a toe. Grrr. I tugged and tugged, until SNAP! The bone broke off.

But then there was a loud *creak!* And a
frightening *crack!* And—uh-oh! The whole
T. rex was breaking apart. Bones crashed to
the floor.

Before my eyes, the T. rex was turning
into a huge cloud of dust. Then I heard more
loud noises.

WOO WOO WOO WOO
the burglar alarm went
off. And up above, Carlotta
Bumblecrumb and Mr. Stubble
shrieked.

I ran to hide.

When the dust settled, I
saw that my rope had wrapped
around their ankles. It had
dragged them through the
roof's open window.
And now they
dangled upside
down, swinging
back and forth.
Their noses just
missed the pile
of bones.

"Get me down!" yelled Carlotta
Bumblecrumb.

I heard a thumping sound and some groans.

Soon I heard police sirens outside the
museum. From my hiding spot, I saw two
cops rush in. They swept their flashlights
across the room.

"What in the world is going on?" said one
police officer.

Their lights stopped at the pile of bones.

The T. rex skull rocked as if it were nodding.

"It's alive!" shouted the other policeman.

No, it was just little old me. I popped up from inside the skull and ran over to the police.

Carlotta Bumblecrumb and Mr. Stubble were nowhere in sight. But I knew they were there. Dogs have great noses.

"WOOF!" I barked. And then I let my great dog nose lead us all to a display of two cave people. "Woof!" I said again, which meant "Check out these buffoons!"—in Dog of course.

One officer took a good look.

"There's something odd about these cave people," he said.

He patted the cave man's fur vest. Dust
flew into the air.

"Ah-ah-ah . . . choo!" Mr. Stubble sneezed.

Carlotta Bumblecrumb groaned.

Mr. Stubble spoke. "Oops," he said. "Sorry
Ms. Bumblecrumb."

"Okay, boneheads," said the policeman.
"You're under arrest."

"Move it, Dumblebum," his partner said.

"It's BUMBLECRUMB!" she yelled. "Can't
anyone get it right?"

One cop hauled the crooks away.

The other patted my head. "Sorry, girl. We have to take you to the animal shelter."

After my recent adventures, that didn't seem so bad.

TA-DA!

The next morning, Helen was in her kitchen.
She was reluctantly looking at photos of cats.

"What about this one?" asked Mom. At the
kitchen table, she held up a cute image of a
kitten. "She's the same color as Martha."

"I guess."

"You could name her Martha," said Mom.

Helen walked to the
fridge. She took down a
drawing of me. "You think
we could train her to fetch?"

Mom frowned. "Well . . ."

Just then, Dad burst in.

"Hey, can you guys give me a hand with the groceries?" he asked.

"Groceries?" said Mom. "But we went shopping yesterday."

"Don't you recall?" said Dad. "I said I might go *by there* on the way home from work?"

He winked.

"Ah!" said Mom. "On the way home from work! That's terrific!"

What's so terrific about groceries?
Helen wondered.

"I'll need help from you two," said Dad.

"Sure," said Mom.

"Okay," mumbled Helen. She looked at her drawing one last time. Then she dropped it into the trash.

Helen shuffled outside after her parents. In the driveway, she peeked into Dad's car.

"There aren't any groceries," she said, confused.

That's when I popped up from the back seat. TA-DA! I'd been waiting there to surprise her.

"Martha!" Helen cried. "You got Martha!"

She opened the car door. She wrapped me
up in a hug. I gave her cheek a slobbery kiss.

"Whee!" shouted Helen, spinning me
around. "Martha, you're home at last!"

And it was true. I was home.

HOME SWEET HOME

When Martha was done talking, the sun had begun to set over the duck pond.

Truman put his pen down.

"Wow," he said. "I can't believe what I've just heard."

"Sorry," said Martha. "That was my stomach. I'm hungry."

"Not that. I'm talking about your interesting background."

Martha looked at her back. "They are nice spots," she said.

89

"No," said Truman. "Your background is all the things that have happened to you in your past," he explained. "What a life story! In the end, all your aspirations came true."

"That's right," Martha said. "It was everything I ever could have hoped for."

"Me, too," said a voice behind her.

Martha turned to see the little red-haired girl. Only she wasn't so little anymore. Just like Martha was no longer a puppy.

"Helen!" cried Martha.

Helen gave her a big hug. Martha licked Helen's cheek.

"If your autobiography is done, dinner is waiting," said Helen.

"Dinner? Yes!" said Martha. "Race you!"

"You bet!" shouted Helen.

"Wait for me!" yelled Truman.

And they all ran home sweet home.

Martha Speaks
GLOSSARY

How many words do you remember from the story?

aspiration: something a person really wants to do

autobiography: the story of a person's life told in that person's own words

background: all the things that happened in the past

flashback: scene in a book, play, movie, or TV program that shows something that happened earlier

narrate: to tell a story

possibility: something that can happen

promising: likely to work out just right

reminisce: to think or talk about things that happened in the past

sequence: order of actions according to when they happen

yearn: to really want

Narrate Your OWN
AUTOBIOGRAPHY

Staple a few sheets of notebook paper down the left side to create your own book. Martha and Truman wrote a few sentences to help you get started.

[your name] 's Amazing Life Story
An Interesting Background

My life story is doggone amazing!

My name is [fill in your name here]. I was born on [birthday] in [city, state]. [Tell funny or interesting story about you as a baby here.]

I have [number] people in my family. They are [names of family members].

I have [number] pets in my family. They include [names and types of pets].

Today I am [age] years old. I am in the [grade] grade at [school]. I live in [city, state]. My friends are [names].

When we're together, we like to [list of favorite activities].

YOU fill in the rest.

My future is full of promising possibilities. The rest of my life story should be doggone amazing, too!

Martha Says,
"Say Cheese!"

Martha has left this empty frame for you. Draw or trace the frame six times on blank sheets of paper. Then draw or paste pictures of yourself at different ages and label them (me as a baby, first day of school, now, future) to illustrate your autobiography. You can even cut and paste the pictures in a different sequence to create flashbacks!